We Have A Baby

Cathryn Falwell

Clarion Books • New York

Clarion Books
a Houghton Mifflin Company imprint
215 Park Avenue South, New York, NY 10003

Printed in China

Library of Congress Cataloging-in-Publication Data

Falwell, Cathryn.
We have a baby / Cathryn Falwell.
p. cm.
Summary: The arrival of a new baby is a cause for celebration,
presenting opportunities to love, watch, touch, and care for
the new family member.
ISBN 0-395-62038-4 PA ISBN 0-395-73970-5
[1. Babies—Fiction.] I. Title.
PZ7.F198We 1993
[E]—dc20
94-40268 CIP AC

LEO 20 19 18 17 16 15
4500251105

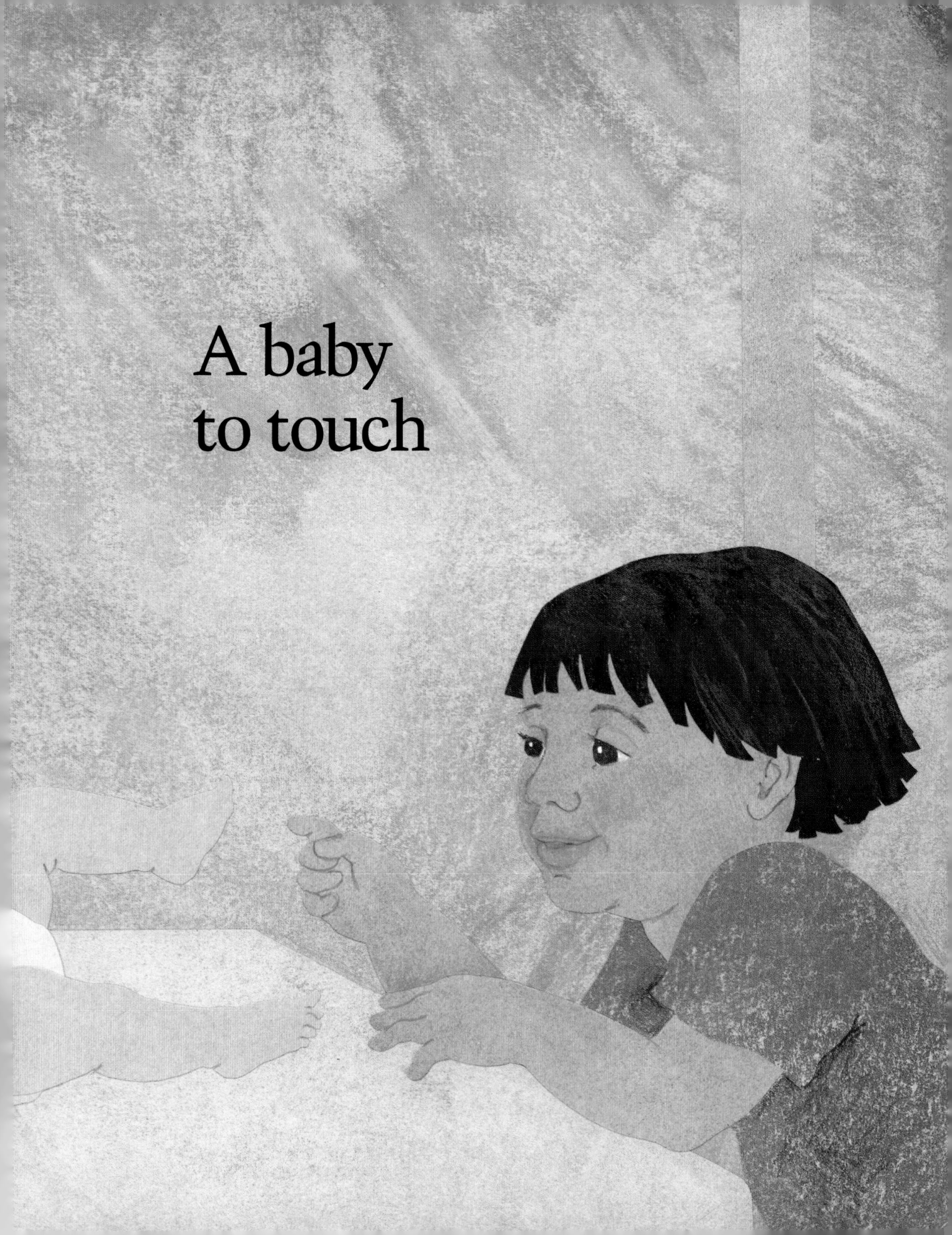

A baby
to touch

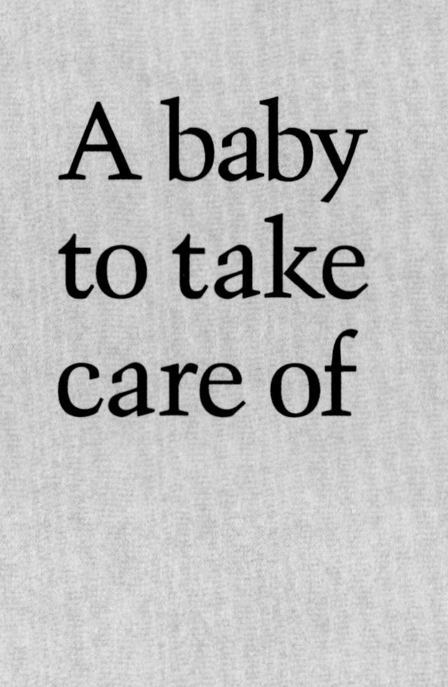

A baby
to take
care of

A baby
to wash

A baby
to dress

A baby
to feed

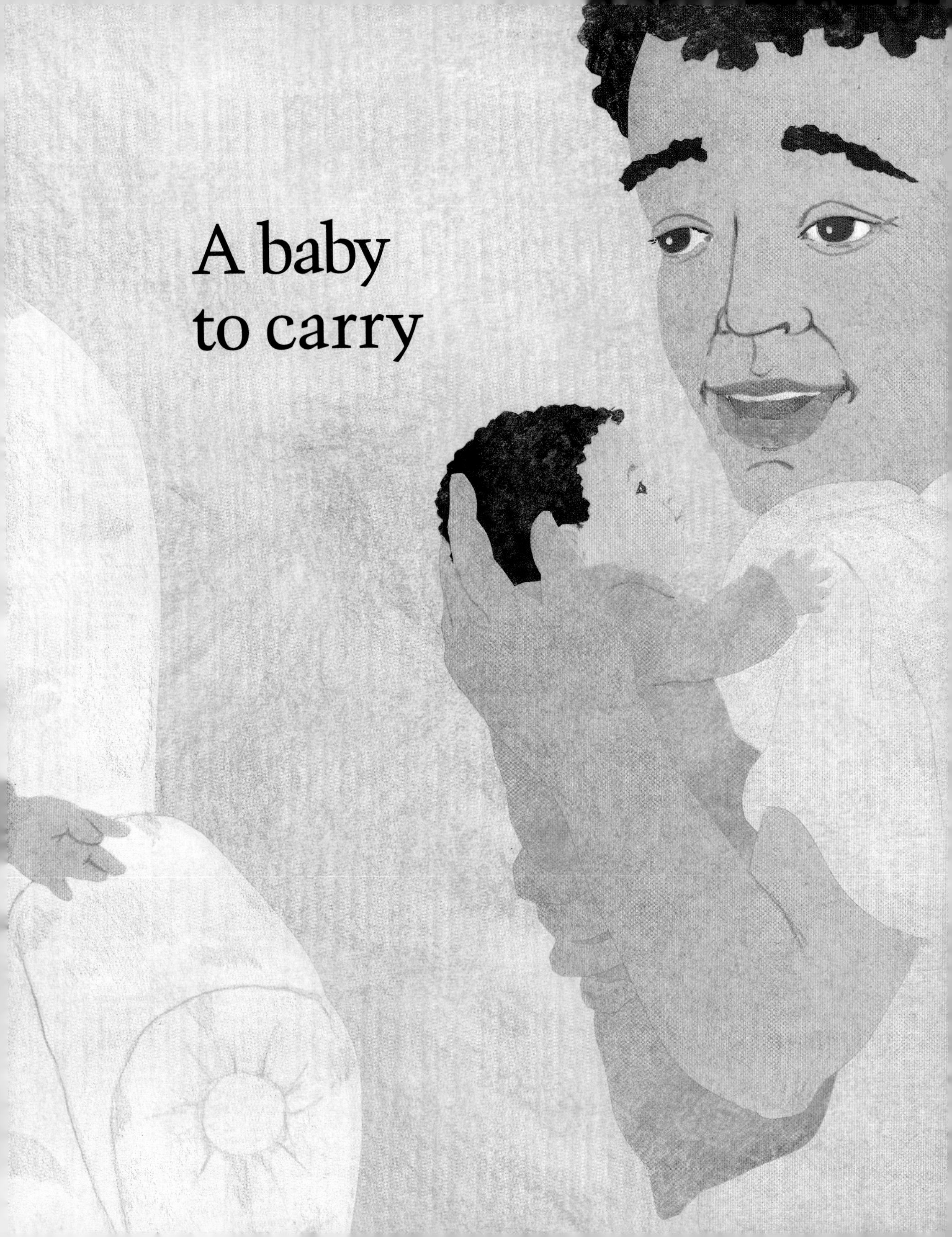

A baby
to carry

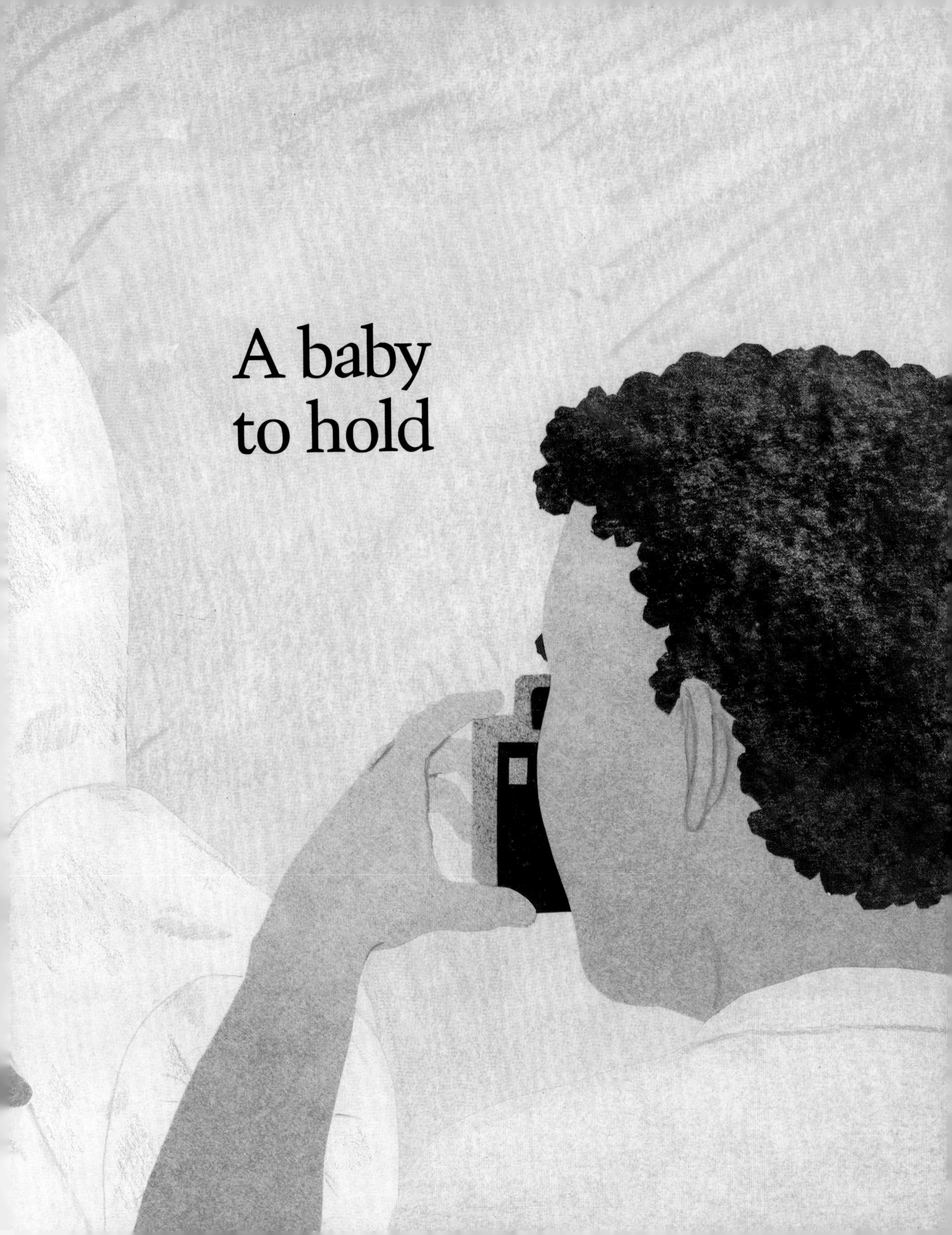

A baby
to hold

A baby
to kiss

A baby
to rock

A baby
to love

A baby who
loves us.